This time the sparks didn't fall.

As the kids watched, the sparks gathered together and formed a ragged line in the air. Slowly, the line drifted down, leaving a shining rectangle in its wake. The rectangle dulled, gradually becoming the color and texture of parchment.

Polly, Sam, and Joe gave a collective sigh of wonder. In the firelight, they could see that the parchment was covered with rows of spiky red letters.

Fire Dreams

THE FOURTH BOOK IN

The Magic Elements Quartet

by Mallory Loehr

A Stepping Stone Book™

RANDOM HOUSE 🏠 NEW YORK

Text copyright © 2001 by Mallory Clare Loehr
Cover art copyright © 2001 by Elizabeth Miles
All rights reserved under
International and Pan-American Copyright Conventions.
Published in the United States by Random House, Inc., New York, and
simultaneously in Canada by Random House of Canada Limited, Toronto.

www.randomhouse.com/kids

Library of Congress Cataloging-in-Publication Data
Loehr, Mallory.
Fire dreams / by Mallory Loehr.
p.   cm. — (Magic elements quartet ; bk. 4)   "A stepping stone book."
SUMMARY: While visiting their grandparents' farm, Joe, Polly, and Sam
are called by the magic of fire to go to Mount Olympus
to repay a debt to Prometheus.
ISBN 0-679-89219-2 (trade) — ISBN 0-679-99219-7 (lib. bdg.)
[1. Brothers and sisters—Fiction.   2. Mythology, Greek—Fiction.
3. Fire—Fiction.   4. Magic—Fiction.]   I. Title.
PZ7.L82615 Fi 2001   [Fic]—dc21   00-51767

Printed in the United States of America   March 2001   10 9 8 7 6 5 4 3 2 1

RANDOM HOUSE and colophon are registered trademarks and
A STEPPING STONE BOOK and colophon are trademarks of Random House, Inc.

To Zoë Allman,
may you have magic always.

Thanks to Rebecca Davis
who read the first draft
of the first Magic Elements book
and made me brave enough to share it.
—ML

Contents

Prologue

He looked into the dancing flames and listened. Through times of darkness and pain, the fire had been his only friend. Now the fire was asking something of him.

He picked up three pieces of metal: one copper, one silver, one gold. He dropped them into the flames, wondering what would happen.

Far away, another fire rose to the call. . . .

CHAPTER ONE

Sparks

The fire roared and stretched toward the night sky. Gold sparks showered like hot raindrops over Sam, Polly, and Joe.

"Yow!" shouted Joe as a spark landed on his arm. He leaned back, and the lawn chair he was sitting in tumbled over.

Polly and Sam didn't even laugh. They were riveted by the fire that towered over them.

"How did it get so big?" Sam wondered.

"Maybe something flew into it," Polly

guessed. "A giant moth or something?"

Joe stood up, staring at the fire, too. "A moth wouldn't do that," he said.

Only moments ago, the three kids had been sitting calmly around the small campfire. Their only thoughts had been of toasting the marshmallows that their father had gone to get. Now the fire crackled over them, spitting sparks and filling the circle of stones that surrounded it.

"Maybe it's a weird kind of wood," Polly said doubtfully.

Joe reached for the bottle of "safety" water they kept nearby in case of emergencies. "I'm going to put it out," he said.

"Wait," said Polly, staring at the dancing colors.

"I think the fire is trying to say something," said Sam.

The fire reached out to them with flickering, many-fingered hands. Then the hands folded into tight fists and suddenly sprang open like flowers blossoming.

Sam and Polly jumped away from the

sparks, kicking over the bench they'd been sitting on. Joe jumped back, too, and fell over the lawn chair with a shout.

This time the sparks didn't fall. As the kids watched, the sparks gathered together and formed a ragged line in the air. Slowly, the line drifted down, leaving a shining rectangle in its wake. The rectangle dulled, gradually becoming the color and texture of parchment.

Polly, Sam, and Joe gave a collective sigh of wonder. In the firelight, they could see that the parchment was covered with rows of spiky red letters.

The fire stretched up and licked the edges of the parchment. They curled up crisp and brown in response. The fire stretched skyward again.

"Stop!" said Polly. She reached out to pull the paper from the air.

The flames got there first, but instead of eating the parchment they gave it a push. As the paper floated into Polly's hands, the logs in the campfire collapsed. The fire sank and settled into the coals with a contented murmur, a wild creature no more.

Sam and Joe crowded around their sister to look at the paper. It was still warm, reminding Polly of a cookie fresh from the oven, except this cookie was the size of the whole cookie pan!

The red letters flickered across the page.

Fire Travel Directions, Part 1:
With first light use copper.
At daylight use gold.
At moonlight use silver.

"Where do you think we're supposed to travel *to*?" wondered Polly.

"Who knows?" grumbled Joe. "The messages never give us any helpful information."

"This one does," argued Sam. "It tells us how to travel by fire."

"Fire," said Polly. "The fourth element." She thought, but didn't say, *This will be the last time*.

Over the past year, the three kids had had magical adventures in water and air. Sam and Polly had also survived an earth adventure with their younger cousin, Audrey.

"At least we know where to start," Polly went on.

"You mean *when* to start," said Joe. "We have no idea *where*."

Polly looked at the message. "What do you mean, *when*?"

"First light," said Joe. "That has to mean dawn, when the sun comes up. That's the first light of the day."

"Oh," said Polly. "I was thinking about the next part." She pointed to the word "copper." "That's *what* we'll need to start."

"We should get the silver and gold, too," said Joe. "Just in case."

"What's copper look like again?" Sam asked.

"It's orangey pink," said Joe.

"Yeah," said Polly. "Like the bottom of the pots and pans we have at home."

"Oh yeah," said Sam.

Joe sighed. "I just wish it told us where we were going."

"That's what you always say," said Polly.

"Well, I always want to know," retorted Joe.

"It says 'Part 1,'" said Sam. "That means there will be a part two. Then we'll know even more!"

Joe nodded. "I guess that's good," he admitted grudgingly.

They sat in silence, thinking their own thoughts, in the cool June night.

The school year had just ended, and the family was visiting the kids' grandparents at their farm. The campfire was at the bottom of a sloping field between the farmhouse and the stream that cut the property in half. From there the kids could see the back of the house. The kitchen window glowed with a buttery light, dimly lighting the back porch.

Above, the moon was a bright crescent. Fireflies twinkled like living sparks. And in their hands was a parchment born of fire with a

mysterious message. It was the perfect beginning for a summer vacation.

"Hey, you all!" came their dad's voice. A
flashlight flicked on as he started down from the
back porch. "Guess who's arrived? Sarah, Ned,
and Little Ed! They'll be down in a few moments along with your mother and Grandma
and Grandpa."

Sarah was their aunt, Ned was their uncle,
and Little Ed was their three-year-old cousin.

While Dad was talking, Sam, Polly, and Joe
hurriedly tried to hide the parchment. But
every time they tried to fold it, it made a crackling sound. Polly finally managed to roll it into
a tube. Then Joe wrapped it in the button-
down shirt he had been wearing over his
T-shirt.

"What's this?" cried their dad when he'd
reached the fire. "You've almost let the fire go
out."

"Sorry," said Sam.

"We were, um, busy, uh, talking," said Polly.

"I'll help," said Joe as their father picked up

a log from the pile several feet away from the fire. Joe grabbed two more.

Together, they brought the fire back to life. Sam and Polly watched the flames suspiciously, but the fire seemed perfectly normal.

"It's too bad Audrey and her mom couldn't come," their father said with a smile. He clapped his hands together with relish. "But it's wonderful everyone *else* is here. The more the merrier!"

The kids nodded weakly. All they wanted was to get started on an adventure. Instead, they watched as the rest of the family came down to the campfire in a cascade of voices and flashlight beams.

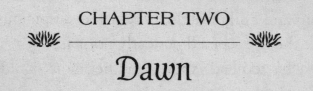

CHAPTER TWO

Dawn

The next morning, Polly was the first to wake. She opened one eye. There was a large flower in front of her. She wondered if she had shrunk, then realized she was looking at wallpaper. She was sleeping on the floor in one of the upstairs bedrooms of the farmhouse. Her parents had gotten the bed, of course, being grownups.

Polly rolled over. The air mattress beneath

her shifted. Everyone had stayed up very late at the campfire, and she was still sleepy. The light coming through the window was orangey pink. She shook her hair out of her eyes and tried to think what it reminded her of.

Copper. Dawn!

Suddenly, Polly was wide awake. She heard a creak and looked under her parents' bed toward the door. She could see Sam's feet, then his knees. Finally, his head appeared as he knelt down and rested it on the floor.

"I'm coming," Polly whispered. She crawled as quietly as she could off the air mattress, around the bed, and out the door. She didn't stand until she was in the hall.

Sam was waiting. Joe was buried in an old quilt on the foldout couch at the top of the landing. Sam had slept there, too. Aunt Sarah, Uncle Ned, and Little Ed were in the other bedroom. A scrabbling sound came from behind their door.

"Maybe the cat got in and wants to get

out," Sam said to Polly as they both looked at the door. "Should we open it?"

"Quietly," said Polly. All they needed was a lot of grownups awake and about.

Sam slowly turned the knob. A mischievous face peeked out—Little Ed.

"Tham!" he squealed.

"Shhh!" Sam and Polly both hissed as Little Ed pushed his round little body through the small space between the door and the door frame. He threw his arms around Sam's waist and then spotted Joe. He let go of Sam and climbed onto Joe's bed.

"Joe!" said Little Ed. "I tickle him!" He wiggled his fingers at the top of the quilt near Joe's neck. Joe pulled the quilt up over his head, but Little Ed was not going to be so easily defeated. He found the edge of the quilt and squeezed under it.

"*Ahhh!*" a squirming Joe shouted as he sat up and threw the quilt off.

Ed had his fingers buried in Joe's armpit.

Joe was trying to pull him off, but he kept laughing.

"Tickle, tickle, tickle!" shouted Little Ed gleefully.

"No tickling!" Joe shouted back between snorts of laughter.

Polly and Sam were laughing, too.

With all the noise, the rest of the family was soon awake.

"So much for sleeping late," said Mom with a raised eyebrow.

Ed started to cry because the tickle game was over. Uncle Ned took him downstairs to start breakfast "before Mother has a chance to do all the work."

Aunt Sarah snagged the upstairs bathroom and everyone else went to get dressed.

Outside, the sky was bright morning blue.

"I guess we missed dawn," said Polly.

"We didn't know what to do yet anyway," said Joe.

"And we have to get the . . . stuff," said

Sam. "You know, the copper and gold and silver."

"Yup," said Joe. "And I think we need to eat a big breakfast, too."

After breakfast, Sam, Polly, and Joe went back upstairs to make a plan of action. Joe had just pulled out the parchment when their mother came out of the bedroom. She had on lipstick and was holding her backpack.

"So what are you all going to do today?" Mom asked, smiling.

"We have a new game," said Polly quickly. "We just made it up."

Joe looked sheepish. He felt too old to even pretend to play games, but he waved the parchment. "Yeah, we're making a treasure map."

"Neat!" said Mom. "Grandma and I are going into town. Your father and Sarah are trimming the trees along the road, and Grandpa is taking the tractor to the garage. If you need anything, Ned's here with Little

Ed. Just tell him if you go anywhere."

"Sure," said Joe.

"And Joe," said Mom, "you're in charge. Be smart."

"Yes, ma'am," Joe said, saluting.

"Ready to go?" Grandma called from downstairs.

"All set," said Mom.

"If you get hungry, there's fruit on the kitchen table," Grandma called up to the kids. "And leftover spaghetti in the fridge."

Sam, Polly, and Joe listened as the front door closed. Then they heard the engine of Grandma's little red sports car start up. As the car drove off, Joe unrolled the parchment.

It was blank.

They all had a moment of shock; then Polly said, "We need the element to see it."

"Of course," said Joe.

The same rule had come with all the magic messages they had gotten.

"I have an idea," he said. He turned the parchment toward the window. The bright sunlight hit it and the words appeared, flickering on the page. "Voilà! The sun is fire."

They studied the directions.

Joe sighed and shook his head.

"No part two," said Sam. "Yet."

"Let's get all the metals," said Polly. "Before the grownups get back."

Joe nodded and rolled the parchment back up. He pointed the tube at Sam. "Silver," he said. "Try the kitchen and dining room."

Sam saluted and went down the stairs.

"That's the easy one," Polly protested.

"He's the youngest," Joe replied. "You can have gold. That shouldn't be too hard. I'll take copper. I'll see if there's anything in the tool-shed."

They went down the stairs together. Then Joe went out the front door, while Polly stood in the hall wondering where to start. Suddenly, she heard a muffled crash from the kitchen. She ran down the hall, hoping Sam hadn't broken anything.

Sam was sitting on the kitchen floor rubbing his head. Every drawer and cupboard was open. Polly could see he'd just banged his head on an open drawer.

"*Oweee*," said Sam, blinking away tears.

"Do you need ice?" asked Polly.

Sam shook his head. "I'm okay," he said. "Look at everything I found! And I haven't even looked in all the cupboards yet."

In the middle of the floor was a pile of shiny utensils and silvery bowls.

Just then Little Ed came in.

"Tham!" he shouted—and bulldozed into the pile.

"No!" yelled Sam and Polly. But it was too late. Silver things crashed and clanged everywhere.

"My drum!" shouted Little Ed as he proceeded to pound on one of the bowls with his fist.

Sam and Polly tried to get him to stop but only managed to replace his fist with a spoon.

Uncle Ned came into the kitchen. "What's going on here?"

"Daddy!" shouted Ed, beating the bowl with each syllable. *"I—play—the drums!"*

"Yeah," said Ned, "and you're doing a great job. Where'd you get that drum?"

"Tham!" shouted Ed. He pointed his spoon at Sam in case there was any confusion.

Polly slipped out of the kitchen as Sam began explaining. She knew he wasn't in trouble. Uncle Ned never got mad at anyone.

Polly stood in the downstairs hall a moment. Then she went into Grandma and Grandpa's bedroom.

It was a cozy room. There was a fan in the window, a faded but pretty rug on the floor, and a quilt Aunt Sarah had made on the bed. The bed was made of dark wood. According to Grandma, it was an antique.

On one of the painted blue walls was a painting Grandma had done of Grandpa when he was young. Around the painting were a bunch of framed photographs. There was a big black-and-white one of Uncle Ned, Mom, and Aunt Jo when they were children; a brownish one of Grandma's mother, Granny, looking haughty; another brownish one of Grandpa's parents, smiling at each other; and many color photos of the grandchildren.

But the best picture was on Grandma's dresser. It was a photo of Grandma and Grandpa's wedding, and it was in a large gold frame. Polly picked up the frame and looked at Grandma's young face, turned toward her grandfather with a happy smile. Grandpa was slim and his hair was combed straight back. It was weird to think of her grandparents being young, even younger than her parents were now.

The frame was heavy in her hands. Polly carefully put it back on the dresser, where it belonged. Then she looked at Grandma's jewelry box. She took a deep breath and opened it, feeling like a thief. It was not a good feeling. She closed the box and left the room.

Where was she going to find something gold? Polly noticed that Ed's clanging had moved from the kitchen to the living room and had been joined by the sounds of Uncle Ned's guitar. Polly went back to the kitchen to check on Sam.

Sam was sitting on the floor, looking at the bottom of a bowl. Many new silvery items had been added to the pile, including a very dented measuring cup, a large serving platter, and several sets of measuring spoons. Sam glanced up when Polly came in.

"Uncle Ned said they aren't all silver," he announced. "If they're silver, it will say it somewhere. That's what he said."

That was another nice thing about Uncle Ned. Unlike other grownups, he never wanted to know *why* you wanted to know something. He just gave you an answer.

Sam put the last bowl down. "The bowls all say 'stainless steel.'"

Polly sat down with him. The two of them started checking the utensils one by one. They all said "stainless steel," too.

"I know Grandma has a set of silver," said Polly.

"What's a set?" asked Sam.

"It's forks and knives and spoons in different sizes, but they all match," said Polly, hoping she was right. "It's what we use at Christmas."

"Look!" said Sam, holding up the large serving platter. "This one says 'silver plate'!" He held it out to Polly upside down.

She looked at the tiny letters stamped on the back. "It says 'silver plat*ed*,'" she said. "I don't think that counts."

Sam's face fell. He moved on to the dented measuring cup.

Polly picked up a giant soup ladle that looked as if it were stained with black ink. It had big letters on its handle, but they were so swirly and curled together that she couldn't tell what they said. The black stains didn't help. She turned it over and searched for little letters. Right where the handle met the curved bowl was a little square stamp and the words "sterling silver."

"Here we go!" she said.

"Really?" asked Sam.

Polly showed him the words.

"I found it at the very back of a drawer," said Sam, taking the ladle back. "I nearly didn't pull it out!"

"Now you can help me find something gold," said Polly.

"Okay," said Sam, waving the ladle.

They stood up and looked at the mess around them.

Polly sighed. "I guess we'd better put all this stuff away first."

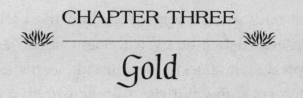

CHAPTER THREE

Gold

Joe was having a hard time in the toolshed. Half of the tools looked as if they'd been sitting there for a hundred years. He was covered in cobwebs, and his hands were greasy. But it wasn't the dirt that was bothering him; it was the wasps.

In one corner of the shed was a wasps' nest that Grandpa was always talking about getting rid of but hadn't ever dealt with. The wasps flew in lazy circles around the hot toolshed. As a result, Joe was moving slowly and carefully.

Joe was going through an old toolbox filled with nails when a wasp landed on the back of his neck. Before he even thought about it, he slapped at it. Luckily, he missed, so his hand didn't get stung. But the wasp flew up in a fury before diving back down. Waving his hands over his head and yelling, Joe ran out of the toolshed.

Sam and Polly looked up as Joe dove through the back door.

"Wasps!" he gasped. He slumped against the door, grimy and sweaty.

Sam smiled and held up the ladle. "Silver!" he said brightly.

"Great," Joe said. He went to the sink and splashed water on his face. Dripping, he grabbed a dish towel. As he did, he saw something that he'd never noticed before. There, hanging on the kitchen wall over the stove, was a shiny orangey pink metal fish.

"I can't believe it!" Joe said. He went over

and took the fish off the wall. "I practically *kill* myself and this copper fish is hanging here the whole time. . . . Why didn't you guys see this?"

"You said look for silver," said Sam. "So I looked for silver."

"And I had gold, except I'm not sure we should take anything that someone might miss," said Polly.

Joe examined the fish. It was hollow.

Polly said, "Let's go ask Ned if we can take it. And the big ladle. And maybe he has something gold he can give us. I didn't think it was right to borrow Grandma's jewelry. I mean, what if we lost it?"

The sound of clanging and guitar strumming had been replaced by light thumps and the voices of Uncle Ned and Little Ed as they sang a made-up song together. Ned's voice was strong and deep, while Ed's voice alternated between a joyful bellow and an uncertain whisper.

Sam, Polly, and Joe went into the living room. Ned was thumping the guitar and humming. Little Ed was whacking the couch with a wooden spoon.

"Can we take these?" asked Joe, holding up the fish and gesturing with it toward Sam's ladle.

Ned looked up and nodded.

"You can take the fish. You can take the spoon. You can take the dish. Just don't take my moon."

"Thanks," said Joe. Grownups were so embarrassing sometimes. "What is this anyway?" he asked. He waggled the fish.

"It's a mold. It's not gold. It can make fish-shaped Jell-O-O-O-O-O-O."

Ed chimed in on the O-O-O's.

"Oh," said Joe, inadvertently adding to the song.

"Speaking of gold," said Polly, raising her voice over the singing, "do you know of something gold we could borrow for a game?"

Ned thumped the guitar absentmindedly and looked up at the ceiling.

"Thing, Daddy!" shouted Little Ed. He

tried to pound on the guitar with the wooden spoon. "Thing to Polly a thong!"

Ned smiled and moved the guitar out of Ed's reach.

"For a niece of mine who's not so old, I can lend a bit of gold."

"Really?" asked Polly. It was such a relief to have someone give her something rather than having to sneak something away.

Ned nodded. Then he stopped strumming and lifted his hands to his ear. He handed Polly the little gold hoop earring he always wore. She held it carefully between her thumb and forefinger.

"Thanks," she said.

Ned nodded.

"I'll be careful with it," she promised.

Sam, Polly, and Joe walked out of the living room. Sam peeked back just in time to see Little Ed whack Uncle Ned with the spoon.

"We're going down the hill to the stream," said Sam.

"Gotcha!" said Ned as he gently wrested the spoon from Ed's little fingers and lifted him onto the couch.

Sam, Polly, and Joe stood around the circle of stones. Joe had on a backpack with sandwiches, water, Band-Aids, matches, the copper fish, and the silver ladle. Sam held the parchment rolled up in his hand. Polly had the gold earring in her pocket.

The hot sun was directly overhead. Their three shadows pooled in small dark puddles at the kids' feet. Joe knelt and made a little fire with sticks they had gathered as they walked down.

Sam unrolled the parchment. He stared at it a moment, then made a choking sound.

"What is it?" asked Polly.

"Something's wrong!" said Sam. He turned the parchment in her direction.

It was blank.

"Turn it toward the fire," said Polly.

"I am!" said Sam. "*And* it's in the sun."

"Let me see it," said Joe.

He grabbed the parchment out of Sam's hands. He tilted it back and forth. It didn't make any difference.

"Let *me* try," said Polly.

"It won't work any better for you," said Joe.

"Can I just see it?" asked Polly. She held out her hand.

"Fine," said Joe.

But as he was handing the paper to Polly, the fire leaped up, as it had the night before. As quick as a snake, it reached out and plucked the parchment from their hands. Then the flames greedily began to devour it.

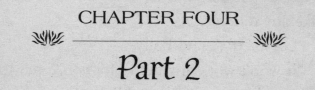

CHAPTER FOUR

Part 2

Polly reached toward the fire, but it was too hot. Joe grabbed a stick and tried to flip the paper out, but the fire wouldn't let it go. It crackled as happily as if it were eating a whole stack of logs.

Sam picked up their bottle of safety water and unscrewed the cap. He was about to throw it on the fire when Joe stopped him.

"It's too late, Sam," he said. "It's gone."

They stared into the fire as the last bit of

the parchment disappeared.

"It must have been hungry," said Sam.

"Yeah, right," said Polly. She looked at Joe. "So what do you want to do now?"

Joe cleared his throat. "Well—"

Just then the flames roared and tossed sparks into the air. The sparks rose and hovered over the fire in a line, just as they had the night before. As the kids watched, the sparks drew a shining rectangle. Seconds later, the fire pushed a new parchment out onto the stones.

Joe knelt and picked up the paper. He turned it carefully to the fire, which had sunk into its bed of twigs.

"This is *not* what it said before," said Joe.

Sam and Polly leaned over his shoulder. This time the writing was bright orange.

Fire Travel Directions, Part 2:
Children of Earth must be accompanied
by a Child of Fire.
Only one journey per CoF.
Multiple travelers permitted.

"What's a CoF?" asked Sam, studying the new directions.

"It's short for 'Child of Fire,'" said Joe. He pointed to the first letter of each word. "See?"

Sam nodded.

"I think *we're* the Children of Earth," said Polly.

"Yeah," Joe agreed.

"But where do we find a CoF?" Polly wondered.

She looked at the fire, as if it could answer.

"What *is* a CoF?" Joe said, thinking.

"A volcano?" asked Sam.

"No," said Joe. "Volcanoes grow out of the earth. Sort of."

"A match," suggested Polly. Then she shook her head. "No, that just makes fire."

Joe gnawed on his lip. Sam scuffed his feet. Polly dug her hands into her pockets. When she did, she felt the little gold earring. She pulled it out with a cry.

"Gold!" she said.

"Uh-huh," said Joe. "So?"

"Gold. And silver and copper. You put them in a fire, and when they're soft enough, you shape them into things."

Light dawned in Joe's eyes. "So what you make out of them is a Child of Fire!"

"Yup!" said Polly. "Like a copper fish, or a silver ladle, or a gold earring!"

Polly looked back at the paper. "We only get one trip from each CoF," she said.

"Now we just have to figure out how to get the fish to take us somewhere," said Joe.

"Wait," said Polly, "maybe it's not the fish we should start with."

"Why not?" asked Sam.

"What did the first note say?" asked Polly.

"Copper at first light," said Joe.

"Daylight is gold," said Polly.

"At moonlight use silver," said Sam.

"Right," Polly said. "Each metal matches the color of the light at a certain time of day."

Sam grinned and nodded. "Yeah!"

Even Joe was pleased. "That makes sense," he said. "That's probably why we remember it."

"It's daylight now," Polly said. "So we should use the earring."

Joe looked up at the sun, wishing he had his sunglasses. "But how are we going to get it to take us somewhere?"

Polly shrugged. "Maybe I should just ask it." She held the earring up to her lips. "Please take us somewhere."

They all looked at the earring expectantly.

Nothing happened.

"Both parchments said fire travel," said Sam. "Maybe we should ask the fire?"

They turned toward the fire.

"Hi, Fire," said Sam. "We're ready to go."

They waited.

Nothing happened again.

"We're ready to go!" Polly said in a louder voice. She held up the earring.

The fire barely crackled in response.

Sam glared at the fire. "You better help us," he said to it sternly.

The fire crackled and leaped a little higher.

"I know!" said Sam. "Let's put the gold *in* the fire!"

"But I only borrowed it!" Polly said. "I can't burn it! How would I give it back?"

She rubbed the little hoop between her fingers. She tried to think of what else she could do that might be magical.

"Come on, Polly," Sam said.

"Just try it," urged Joe.

"Please?" said Sam.

Polly sighed and shook her head. She looked at the earring one more time. "Oh, all right," she said. "But I'm not going to just throw it in." She looked around.

"What do you want to do?" asked Joe.

"I need a stick to put it on," said Polly. "Then I'll hold it in the fire."

"Here," said Sam. He handed her a long twig.

Polly slipped the earring onto the twig.

They all looked at the small golden hoop dangling from the wood.

Then Polly slowly put the twig into the fire. For a moment the earring just sat there on the burning twig. Then all the flames of the fire bent in as if they were looking at it, too.

The little circle of gold quivered, then started to blister.

"I hope the earring can't feel anything!" cried Polly. She started to pull it out.

"It's not alive," Joe said.

"How do you know?" asked Polly. But she held the stick where it was.

The earring swelled. Slowly, it pushed itself off the twig, falling into the fire. They all leaned closer to watch the misshapen blob of gold. Guarded by leaping flames, the blob grew into a golden bubble. When it had reached the size of an egg, it jumped out of the fire.

The kids leaped out of the way, bumping into each other. The golden egg grew and grew, first out, then up. They watched, breathless, as it stretched taller than Sam, then Polly, then Joe—but only by an inch or two.

The molten gold flashed in the sun as two

arms emerged from the sides. Then the bottom half separated into two legs. Finally, an egg shape pushed its way out of the top on a skinny neck. It looked a little like C-3PO, the gold robot from *Star Wars*.

Delicate ears fanned out from the head. Lips and a nose formed, then a pair of closed eyes, each with a fringe of gold lashes that lay on a gold cheek.

There was a whirring sound. Then the eyes opened with a click.

CHAPTER FIVE

❧⟍ ———————————— ❧⟍

Fire Child

Sam, Polly, and Joe took a step back. The gold man's eyes were emerald green and glowing as if lit from behind.

The eyes blinked again, looking straight ahead; then the head swiveled smoothly around to take in the surroundings: the green field, the forest in the distance, the farmhouse on the hill.

"What is this?" asked the robot. His voice

tinkled a little, like a low-pitched music box. "What's going on?"

"Um, we sent for you," said Polly. "I think. Are you a Child of Fire?"

The head tilted down to look at the three kids. They looked back expectantly.

"Humans!" said the robot, not answering Polly's question. "And little ones." The faint metal whirring sound came again as he scanned the horizon. He waved his hands in a vague but agitated manner. "I really must get back. Very pressing business I have there. Very pressing."

"But I think you have to help us," said Polly.

"Help *you?*" the robot snapped. He shook his head. "No. *You* have to help *me*. You brought me here, wherever here is. And now you must return me to my rightful home." His hands flapped again, reminding Polly of a bird.

"We don't know how," said Sam. He was confused. The robot was definitely magical, but magical beings were supposed to be helpful and smart, not nervous and snappy.

"Don't know what the world is coming to," the robot muttered. "Little humans should never be given power. No ability to see what's important and what's not."

Joe's eyes narrowed. "Hold on!" he said. "You don't know us, or what we're doing." He paused a moment, realizing that they didn't know what they were doing either. "Are you a Child of Fire?"

"Yeah," Sam said. "We're supposed to do something with fire."

"Really," the robot replied in a withering tone. "Well, no one asked me."

"We *couldn't* ask you," said Joe. This was frustrating. The robot was not half as impressive as he looked. "We didn't know you were coming either," Joe went on, thinking that if they *had* known the robot was coming, they would have asked for someone else.

The robot wasn't paying attention. He was looking at the fire with disapproval. "I can tell you one thing—that fire needs more fuel," the robot said. "Don't you know how to feed it?"

"Aha!" said Polly. "That *proves* you're a Child of Fire."

"What *are* you going on about?" asked the robot.

Polly sighed and decided to try a different approach. "You're so shiny and beautiful," she said. "You *must* be from somewhere special."

The robot smirked stiffly. "Mount Olympus," he said proudly. "The home of the gods. I was made by the god Hephaestus in his very own forge."

"What's a forge?" asked Sam.

The robot sighed. "You poor ignorant child. A forge is where metal is worked."

"Is there fire in it?" asked Sam.

"Yes," said the robot curtly. "I was made in Hephaestus' forge, which is why I am so extraordinary."

The three kids looked at each other with raised eyebrows.

"I am one of Hephaestus' most trusted

children," the robot continued, happy to talk about something familiar. "I have a silver tongue, and I can think all by myself."

"Not very well," muttered Joe.

The robot swiveled its head. "I heard that, you inferior being," he said.

"Can I see it?" asked Sam.

"See what?" said the robot.

"Your silver tongue," answered Sam.

The robot looked as if he wanted to say no, but pride took over. He stuck out his tongue. It was silver.

"Cool!" said Sam.

"Thank you," the robot said with a nod. Compliments definitely cheered him up.

"Listen," said Joe through gritted teeth. He held out the parchment. "This came out of the fire. We're just trying to follow directions, but they aren't very clear. You are obviously *way* smarter than we are, so perhaps you can read it and tell us what to do, and then you can be on your way."

The flattery worked, despite the sarcasm.

"Very well," said the robot. He took the parchment and glanced at it. "Oh dear," he said. "Oh dear."

"What?" asked Polly. "What?"

The robot looked at the sky. "Why do these things always happen to me?"

"What are you talking about?" asked Joe.

The robot looked at the fire. He gave a humming sigh. "It would help if it were bigger."

"Huh?" said Sam.

"I think we all have to fit," said the robot. He sounded nervous again, as if he didn't really know what he was doing.

"In the fire?" asked Polly.

"Well, how else did you expect us to get anywhere?" snapped the robot, lashing out in his nervousness. "What did you think that 'fire travel' meant?"

"I don't know," Polly answered in a small voice. "Maybe in a nice chariot or something?"

The robot snorted.

"Where are we going?" asked Sam.

"Wherever the fire takes us," said the robot.

Joe threw a log on the fire. "You don't have to come with us," he said.

"I believe I do," said the robot sourly, holding out the parchment. "Note the second line."

The three kids reread the second line, which stated: "Children of Earth must be accompanied by a Child of Fire."

The robot fanned the flame with a shining hand. The fire sprang higher. Sam and Polly glanced at each other.

"Maybe this isn't such a good idea," said Polly. She believed in magic, but what she knew about fire made it hard to feel comfortable stepping into it.

"Is there any way to test this?" asked Joe.

The robot shook his head. "Not to my knowledge."

"And you don't know where we're going," Joe confirmed.

The robot shook his head again. "Unfortunately not," he replied. "Fire magic is the most temperamental and unpredictable of the elemental magics. It has to follow rules, but it tends to find ways around them."

"Oh dear," said Polly.

"As long as you're with me, the fire travel should work," said the robot. "But I wouldn't try it alone if I were you."

"Oh, *really*," said Joe sarcastically. He opened his mouth to say something else, but Polly nudged him.

"Don't make him mad," she whispered. "We need him."

Joe bit his lip and remained silent.

The three kids looked into the fire, which now filled the protective circle of stones. The flames danced and waved hypnotically. The many-fingered hands reached out to them, beckoning. They stepped toward it.

The fire leaped.

"Perfect," said the robot. He stepped into the flames.

The fire rose around him.

"Come on," the robot said impatiently.

"Let's get this over with." He put out a hand wreathed in fire and grabbed Joe.

Joe struggled for a moment, then gave up and stepped into the fire beside the robot. He winced. It reminded him of stepping into water that was hot enough to feel unpleasant, but not hot enough to really burn. Joe looked out of the fire at Sam and Polly.

The robot reached out again and pulled them in as well. The heat was like hot sunlight. The flames tickled them.

"Remember, don't try this alone," said the robot.

They had one last glimpse of the farm, glazed golden green by the curtain of fire. Then it was gone and they were standing in a fire at the edge of the mouth of a volcano.

CHAPTER SIX

Cyclops

A loud clanging sound rang out, as if a giant Little Ed were down in the volcano banging on a bowl. Sparks jumped like cheap fireworks into the air. Small fires blossomed around them, and smoke—or was it steam?—coiled into the clear blue sky.

The robot pulled them out of the fire onto a clear patch of shiny black ground. "It's not as bad as I thought," he said.

"Yeah, this is great," Joe said. "Nothing like a volcano for comfort."

The volcano sloped a long way down to a stunning blue ocean. In the distance another volcano-shaped island rose out of the water wreathed in clouds.

"It's so big!" said Sam. The hole in the top of the volcano was the size of a lake.

They all peered into the volcano. A huge, craggy stone staircase spiraled straight down from where they stood, into a pit of molten lava a mountain's length below. The lava glowed and bubbled like spaghetti sauce in a pot.

"Are we supposed to go down there?" Polly asked.

"Indeed," said the robot. He frowned. "There you will find my father's other work-shop. He might be able to help."

Joe was relieved to at least know where they were going, even if it wasn't clear why. They all looked down into the volcano again. They couldn't tell if the staircase went directly into the lava or if it went into a passage above it. The staircase itself looked as if it had been carved from a single column of stone.

Suddenly, the clanging sound stopped, and they could hear the bubbling and hissing of lava.

"Let's do it," said Joe.

Polly went first.

The stairs were massive. Each one was several feet wide and shaped like a slice of pie. The stone was very uneven, and there was no railing to hold on to, so Polly went slowly. Sam followed and Joe went after him.

"You don't have to be so careful!" Joe called.

"I don't want to fall!" Polly called back. "So don't yell at me!"

As they went down one craggy step at a time, the daylight disappeared. It was replaced by the red-gold glow of the lava and sparks. The air got hotter. Joe wondered if they were wrapped in some kind of magical protection that kept them from dying of heat.

Joe looked back the way they'd come. The

staircase towered above him, but to the side he could see the rim of the volcano. It was black, accenting the blueness of the sky. A shape was silhouetted against the blue. It was the robot.

"Hey!" Joe called. "Aren't you coming?"

"No, thank you!" shouted the robot. "I never go belowground. I am a creation of Olympus. Just tell my father that I'm here and need to get home, please."

Suddenly, the robot looked over his shoulder. He gave a start. The next moment he had disappeared from Joe's sight. Joe heard footsteps hurrying toward him.

"What is it?" asked Joe when the robot reached him.

"Oh, nothing," said the robot, "just a little, ahem, Cyclops."

"A Cyclops?" said Joe. "Like one of those dudes with one eye?"

"Exactly like," said the robot. "We must hurry!" He pushed past Joe, nearly knocking him into the lava below.

"Hey!" Joe shouted angrily.

But the robot was already galloping ahead.

Joe glanced back up to the volcano edge. Sure enough, a huge, shaggy head was peering—glaring?—over the black rim. Even in the dark, Joe could see the bright yellow eye in the middle of its forehead. A humongous hand rose beside the head.

Joe didn't wait to see what the hand would do. He turned and began running down the bumpy steps as fast as he could. A fire was one thing, but a Cyclops was another.

Sam and Polly turned to see the robot coming right at them. "Quickly, quickly," he said, waving his arms.

"Where's Joe?" asked Sam.

The robot didn't answer. He just pushed past Sam and Polly and bounded on down.

Sam and Polly ran back up the stairs just in time to see Joe slip. His arms flapped as he tried to catch himself. But the staircase curved and he went off. At the last minute, though, he turned and caught the edge of the step with one hand. He hung on, his feet dangling.

"Help!" he yelled.

"Joe!" screamed Polly.

Sam ran up the stairs with Polly. By the time they reached him, Joe had his other hand on the edge of the stair. Polly grabbed one of his wrists and Sam grabbed the other.

"Pull!" shouted Polly.

Together they pulled, struggling to brace themselves. Joe seemed to weigh a ton. Sam could feel his brother's arms straining to help them. They couldn't lift him.

"Can you bring your leg up?" Polly yelled. Sweat dripped down one side of her face.

"Okay," Joe grunted.

They felt him struggle. One leg appeared on a step below them. Then it slipped off. Joe groaned.

"Where's that robot when you need him?" muttered Polly. "Don't let go, Joe!"

She lay on the step and inched her hands down. She could just barely grab Joe's T-shirt. And that was when she felt the backpack strap.

"Joe!" she called. "I'm going to pull on the

backpack so you're not so heavy. Then you try to get your leg up again."

Joe moaned.

"Sam, you go down and grab his leg," said Polly.

Sam moved down to where Joe's leg had come up.

Polly pulled on the heavy backpack. She felt Joe's arms tense and his body twist as he lifted his leg to the step. Sam grabbed his foot and held it.

"I can't do it!" said Joe.

"Yes, you can!" said Polly.

"You can!" said Sam, clinging to Joe's ankle, trying to pull it.

Polly felt Joe's fingers loosening. "*No!*" she shouted.

Sam looked up to see a gigantic black shape leaning over Polly. He shut his eyes. The next thing he knew he was dangling from Joe's foot in the hot air, hanging on for dear life.

Joe's eyes were also shut. For a moment he felt as if he were being stretched up and down at the same time. Something heavy was hanging from his foot. Something else was pulling on his arms.

Then all three kids were in a gasping heap on the stairs.

Polly had her arms around Joe's neck. Sam was still gripping his foot. Joe pulled himself up and saw the large yellow eye hovering over him. Giving a little sigh, he fainted.

Polly felt Joe go limp and wondered what had happened. She pushed herself up to see who had rescued them.

Blinking at her was an eyeball as big as her head.

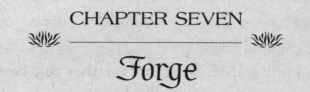

CHAPTER SEVEN

Forge

The eye backed away. Polly could see that it nearly filled a giant forehead in a face taller than she was. The face had a squashed nose and a wide mouth with big teeth that looked red in the lava light. Shaggy hair sprang from the creature's head in all directions. His body was a crouching, dense shadow filling the staircase. His feet, with large, sooty toes, took up several steps.

The Cyclops raised a hand in a careful gesture, his fingers curling into a tentative wave. His hand was as big as his face. "So sorry so scary," he said. Long eyelashes swooped over the eye and back up.

Polly gulped. She heard another gulp beside her. It was Sam. She looked at her brother. Except for the snot running down his face, he looked fine. He wiped his nose with his arm, staring up at the Cyclops.

Polly turned back to the giant man. His huge hand was still up. She was rather touched that he was trying so hard not to scare them.

"That's okay," she said, smiling as kindly as she could. Just then Joe shifted beside her.

The Cyclops pointed at Joe. "I scare him. He see me. He close his eyes and fall over."

"Joe fainted?" said Sam.

The Cyclops nodded.

"I can't believe it!" said Sam. He laughed. It felt good to laugh after being so scared.

"I bet he won't believe it either," said Polly, also laughing, as much from relief as from the thought of Joe keeling over. After all, he'd already nearly fallen into a pit of burning lava. The Cyclops was probably just one thing too many for him.

"Here to see Smith?" asked the Cyclops.

"Who?" asked Polly.

"Smith," answered the Cyclops. "*The* Smith," he added meaningfully.

"We're here to see Hi-Hephaestus," Sam said, managing the pronunciation.

The Cyclops nodded his shaggy head. "The Smith," he repeated. "We go." He carefully pushed his legs out in front of him, so that he was sitting on the big staircase. His legs hung off into the volcano.

Polly and Sam had to squish over to one side, pulling Joe with them. "What are you doing?" Polly asked.

"I slide down," said the Cyclops happily.

"Like a sled!" said Sam.

The Cyclops picked Joe up and slung him over his shoulder, backpack and all. Joe looked as tiny as a kitten.

"Hold on a sec," said Polly. "Let me carry the backpack."

"Backy pack?" said the Cyclops, turning and looking at his own back.

"The thing on Joe's back," said Polly. "The bag."

"Oh," said the Cyclops. He held Joe up with one hand and helped Polly take the backpack off him.

"It's a good thing that we didn't lose it," said Polly.

"Or lose Joe," said Sam.

"Or lose Joe," Polly agreed with a shiver.

"I carry Joe *and* backy pack," said the Cyclops. He slung Joe back over one shoulder and put the heavy pack over his wrist like a tiny purse.

"Thanks," said Polly. Then she stuck out her hand. "I'm Polly."

The Cyclops looked surprised. He stuck out the hand with the backpack. "Me Dimitri."

"Nice to meet you, Dimitri," Polly said politely. She shook one of his fingers in both hands.

It sounded strange to have formal introductions inside a volcano, but the Cyclops seemed pleased. He nodded his head and smiled, showing all his giant teeth.

"Me Sam," said Sam. He put his hand out as well.

"Nice to meet you, Sam," said Dimitri, beaming. He looked down the stairs and seemed to be thinking.

"What is it, Dimitri?" asked Polly.

"An idea," he answered. "Me carry Joe and backy pack *and* Polly and Sam!" As he said their names, he lifted Polly onto his other shoulder and held Sam like a baby on his arm.

Polly wrinkled her nose. Sitting on the Cyclops was like sitting on a hairy, smelly couch. She would have been happier walking, but she didn't want to disappoint Dimitri, not when he seemed so happy.

Sam didn't mind the smell or feel, but as

the Cyclops started to slide down the stairs, he was jounced around uncomfortably. The Cyclops curled his arm around the inside wall to guide himself as they spun down. Polly had to twist her hands in Dimitri's shaggy hair to keep from falling off. Compared with the sweaty smell of the giant's skin, the smoky smell of his hair was rather nice and reminded her of a barbecue. She tried not to look over the edge.

The stairs wound into the side of the volcano in what seemed like an impossible way. There was a large opening in the rock, which Dimitri flew through. It was very dark.

The Cyclops stood, still holding the three kids. He started walking down, although neither Polly nor Sam could see the stairs, which must have been huge for Dimitri to fit. The only thing visible was something small and red and glowing far below. As they neared it, it grew bigger, until Sam could see that it was a curtain of lava, like the curtain of water behind a waterfall.

The Cyclops plunged through it. Sam noticed that the hot ooze actually squeezed to one side for Dimitri automatically, like an elevator door. Past the lava curtain was a cavernous octagonal room with sweeping ceilings. It was so big Dimitri fit standing up. Polly looked down. She was as high up as if she were standing on the roof of a small house. The Cyclops put Sam and Polly down on their feet. They looked around.

There were fireplaces in every wall. A set of shining silver hammers hung beside each of the fireplaces, arranged from giant to tiny. Stacks of wood were piled high beside several fires. There was also an oversized wood stove big enough for several people to fit in. Inside it a fire burned.

The whole room glowed red from the fires. The floor was shiny black. Altogether, it should have felt scary, but instead it gave the kids a feeling of warm happiness.

The feeling might have come from the man who sat on a heavy iron chair in the center of the room. The chair was like a throne, and beside it was a table piled high with bits of metal and sparkling gems. The man's shoulders were broad, his arms heavily muscled, and his skin black with soot. In one huge hand was a tiny hammer. In the other was a delicate chain of gold links.

"Smith!" cried Dimitri. "Here are Sam and Polly and Joe and a backy pack!" He dropped the backpack and gently lowered Joe from his shoulder into a lumpy pile on the floor.

The man's hairless head glowed in the firelight. His smile—a wide-open smile—glowed, too, for all of his teeth were gold.

"Very good, Dimitri!" said Smith. He ran his hands along the sides of the iron chair and it moved forward. It was a wheelchair.

A gold head peeked out from behind the wheelchair. The robot moved along with it as it rolled forward, using it like a shield. "*I'm* the one who brought them," the robot whined.

The Cyclops took a step forward. The robot cowered and ducked back behind the wheelchair. "Don't let it hurt me," came the music-box voice.

The bald man sighed. "He won't hurt you, Junior. He has *never* hurt you," he said with infinite patience, his head turned back to address the robot.

The robot, Junior, didn't answer.

The bald man shrugged and looked at Polly and Sam. "I think being in Olympus has made him a little, well, *intolerant* of things that are beautiful in ways that aren't obvious. He hates to come down here. Although you'd think that knowing *me* . . ." Smith gestured toward his legs.

They were as twisted and gnarled as ancient tree roots.

"Ah, the plight of a parent," he went on. He chuckled and looked up through bushy black eyebrows. "But that's enough moaning! Welcome to my forge! Dimitri and I were taking a little break. His two brothers are on vacation, so we're taking it a bit easy."

Dimitri grinned and nodded. "Having fun," he explained.

Sam stepped forward and looked the bald

man in the eye. "Are you Hephaestus?" he asked.

"That I am," the man replied. "But you can call me Smith, just like most people do these days. As in blacksmith, silversmith, goldsmith, and so on. I am the smith of all metals."

"A common name," came a mutter from behind the chair.

Smith smiled his golden smile. "That it is. But it is also an honest one."

Just then Joe stirred.

"You wake up, Joe?" asked Dimitri. "Joe?"

Joe heard a booming voice calling to him. He lifted his head. "Huhhhh?" he moaned. His whole body hurt, and he didn't want to wake up, even more than usual.

Sam and Polly went over to him.

"You're okay, Joe," said Polly. "You're just a wimp."

Sam put a hand on Joe's shoulder. "Uhhh," said Joe. His shoulders felt as if his arms had been pulled out of their sockets.

"What was I thinking?" said Smith. He

called to the Cyclops, "Dimitri, fetch a cushion." He rolled the wheelchair, the robot scuttling behind it, to one of the great black fireplaces that ringed the room. This fireplace had a bunch of pots and one teakettle suspended over it from an iron bar. Smith pulled the teakettle down and held it up. "Hold this, please, Junior," he said.

Junior stuck out a gold hand and took the teakettle, then whisked it behind the wheelchair.

Smith then took a cup and a small black box off a low shelf beside the fire.

Dimitri lifted Joe easily onto a plump cushion the size of a small mattress. It was covered with a fine mesh of steel gray, and Joe was surprised by its softness.

Sam and Polly watched Smith tap some gold flakes from the box into the cup. He held the cup out.

"A little water, please," he said.

Junior's arm stuck out with the teakettle in the direction of the cup. But when he tipped the kettle, the water missed and spilled on the floor.

Smith looked at the puddle of water and shook his head. "This nonsense must stop," he said. The words could have been sharp, but Polly noticed how gently they were spoken. "Please come out and stop behaving badly, Junior."

Junior shuffled out from behind the chair and poured several drops of water into the cup. He handed Smith a spoon from the shelf.

Smith stirred the mixture. Then he rolled over to Sam and Polly, holding out the cup with the spoon still in it. "Joe needs to swallow this," he said. "But he has to eat it from the spoon, not from the cup."

Polly took the cup. It was gold with a large turquoise embedded in the side. The handle of the spoon looked like an iron twig. Inside the cup the gold flakes had become a golden paste. Polly scooped some up in the spoon and went over to Joe.

Dimitri knelt down and lifted Joe's head with a giant hand.

"Joe," said Polly.

He groaned.

Polly rolled her eyes. "Stop being a baby," she said.

Sam knelt beside her. "Come on, Joe."

Joe opened one eye.

"We're at Hephaestus' forge, only he's called Smith," said Sam.

Joe opened his mouth to say something, and Polly shoved in the gold paste. Joe nearly spit it out. Then he changed his mind and swallowed. He licked his lips and opened his mouth again. Whatever it was, it was delicious.

Polly put another spoonful in Joe's mouth. He swallowed again, the delicious taste followed by a delicious warmth that spread through his aching body. By the third swallow, his body had stopped hurting. He reached out to take the cup and spoon from Polly.

She handed them to him. Joe was disappointed to discover that there was only one spoonful left. He savored the last morsel. Then he looked around.

Sam and Polly were beside him. A big bald man in a black wheelchair was behind them. The obnoxious robot stood next to the chair. He knew there was one other thing he was looking for. He turned his head to the side and saw a giant finger. Then the eye appeared beside him.

"Hello, Joe," said Dimitri. "Don't go back to sleep. I be your friend."

Joe smiled. The gold paste seemed to have helped more than just his body.

"His name is Dimitri," said Sam. "And he made you faint!"

"No, I didn't," said Joe, sitting up. "I passed out from exhaustion."

"I don't think so," said Polly with a giggle. "You were scared silly."

"Well, it's his fault if I was," said Joe, pointing at the robot. "He was running away from him."

"That's not tr—" began the robot defensively.

"Enough," said Smith in his soft, firm voice. He turned to Sam, Polly, and Joe. "Tell me your story."

The three kids showed him the second parchment they had. Then they told him about the first parchment, finding the metal objects, the second parchment, and how the robot had appeared and helped them travel through the fire to the volcano. They explained how they had gone down the staircase and met Dimitri.

When they finished, Smith rubbed his chin. "I see a few problems ahead," he said.

CHAPTER EIGHT

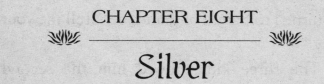

Silver

"What do you mean you see a few problems?" Joe asked suspiciously.

"You didn't go in the order of the first set of directions," Smith answered.

All three kids opened their mouths to defend their actions. But Smith raised his hand, and their mouths shut. "You may have scrambled the magic," he went on.

After a moment, Polly spoke. "What do you mean we 'didn't go in the order'?"

"You didn't start at dawn," Smith replied. "You skipped it and worked the day magic."

"What's going to happen?" asked Sam.

Smith shrugged his big shoulders. "I'm not sure," he said. "Riddles aren't my strong point. I'm a straight thinker, not a twisted one."

The kids were quiet again.

"Might I make a suggestion?" Junior asked. His words were polite, but his tone implied that the rest of them were idiots.

"Speak," said Smith with a smile.

Junior waved his hand at the fire beside him. "Put the parchment in there. At least we'll find out what comes next."

"I don't know about that," said Joe, looking dubiously at the fire. "The fire really chose when to do the parchment things. We didn't make it happen."

"We have to put the silver ladle in a fire next," said Sam. "When the moon comes up."

"Yeah," said Polly. "Then I bet a silvery Fire Child will be made and then we can fire-travel again."

"Do you know where we're going?" Joe asked Smith.

Smith shook his head. "I am the one who helped the fire with the magic. But I don't know what is intended." He looked into one of the big fires. "The moon should be rising about now. Perhaps you should go aboveground and try out some of your ideas."

"Why can't we do it here?" asked Joe.

"There's no moonlight down here," scoffed the robot. "Obviously, you need natural light for these things to work."

"I thought the firelight would be enough," said Joe.

"I believe Junior is right," said Smith. "You will need the light of both fire and the moon."

Joe looked up. "I guess that means we should go."

"I will stay here," said Smith. "But Junior and Dimitri will go with you to the top. There are plenty of fires up there."

"Yes, yes," said the Cyclops. "And I won't forget the backy pack."

The moon was a bright crescent, but it left enough darkness in the sky for the stars to shine sharply. Three human kids, a gold robot, and a Cyclops stared up at it from the mouth of the volcano. Their faces were lit with the golden red light.

Joe turned away and looked around at the little fires on the dark ground. One looked bigger than the others. Joe walked over to it.

Another fire a few feet away made a snapping sound. Joe glanced over. It was a smaller fire, but brighter and livelier.

"Let's use that fire," he called.

"Yes," said Junior. Joe was startled to find the robot was right next to him.

"It seemed like it was talking," Joe said to him, feeling a little sheepish.

"I know," Junior replied in his usual haughty voice. "I heard it, too."

Sam, Polly, and Dimitri came up. The Cyclops squatted down to look at the fire, which was the size of two of his toes put together. Sam was struggling to pull the ladle out of the back-pack.

"Let me help," said Polly impatiently.

She grabbed on to the backpack while Sam wrestled the ladle out. He held it up.

"Let's give it a try," said Joe.

"Here goes," said Sam. He held the ladle in the fire.

"Let go of it!" snapped Joe. "Or—"

"Yeow!" shouted Sam, dropping the ladle into the fire as the heat traveled up its long handle. He popped his fingers in his mouth.

"Told you," said Joe.

They all watched as the ladle turned black in the fire. They waited for something to happen.

Two minutes passed, then five.

"Nothing's happening," said Sam. He was disappointed.

"Did we ruin the magic?" Polly asked worriedly.

"Let's try and be patient," said Joe. "The magic wants us to do something, so it should help." But he was a little concerned himself. If they'd *really* messed up, how long would it take them to get back home?

More minutes passed.

"Not good," said Dimitri.

Just then the little fire crackled and sent a shower of sparks in his direction.

"Let's get the parchment out," said Joe. "Maybe that's what it wants."

Polly took the parchment from the backpack. She held it out to the fire, as if it were a bone and the fire a stray dog. But the fire didn't reach for it, as it had before. Instead, it kept spitting sparks in Dimitri's direction. The Cyclops seemed unbothered.

"Don't the sparks hurt?" Polly asked.

"Not me," said the Cyclops, "too tough."

"It's not toughness," said Junior. "He was an Earth Child but fire adopted him as well, because he has worked with my father for so long."

An idea sprang into Joe's mind. "Are you saying that Dimitri is a Fire Child?" he asked.

"I am Child of Earth and Fire," said Dimitri.

"How can you be both?" Sam asked.

The Cyclops looked confused. "Just am."

"It's like people who are from one country and move to another," said Joe. "Like someone can live in America and be American, but their family originally came from China or Mexico or Africa or Ireland."

"Oh, I get it," said Sam. "I want to be from two places, too."

"May we return to the problem at hand?" asked the robot.

"Fine," said Joe. "Here's what I was thinking. If Dimitri is a Fire Child, then he ought to be able to help us fire-travel to wherever we have to go next."

"I fire-travel you?" asked Dimitri, beaming.

"I think so," said Joe. He looked at Polly and Sam.

They both nodded.

"He should hold us while he steps into the fire," said Polly. "In case it doesn't work."

"But I thought that we all had to be *in* the fire," said Sam. "That's what Junior said."

"He doesn't know everything," said Joe. "For all we know, he could have stepped into the fire and just touched us."

"What I did made perfect sense to me," said the robot. "But go ahead, try it *your* way. Just don't blame me if things don't work out."

Joe looked up at the hulking Cyclops. "How's it sound to you, Dimitri?"

"Sounds good," said the Cyclops, his smile as big as his one eye.

"I wonder about the silver, though," said Polly, looking at the blackened ladle in the fire.

"The magic is scrambled," Joe reminded her. "Who knows how it was supposed to work."

"Well," said Junior, "I will leave you here. Now that everything is under control."

Just then the fire rose with a crackle. It reached out to the parchment in Polly's hand.

"No!" said Polly. She instinctively pulled the paper out of the fire's reach.

"Give it to the fire!" said Joe.

"Oh, right," said Polly.

The fire stretched its flames over as if it were being blown toward Polly. The second she held the parchment out, the flames ate it.

Again they waited and watched the fire. Junior tapped his foot impatiently.

They waited for another parchment to rise. Instead, the fire danced around the blackened ladle, which began to shed the darkness like a snake shedding skin. Soon it was shiny and silver again. Then the fire sunk low, burning a hot blue.

"Weird," said Joe.

"I suggest pulling it from the flame," said Junior.

Dimitri plucked the ladle from the fire. It looked like a sewing needle between his big fingers. He delicately passed it to Junior.

The robot gave the Cyclops a startled look but took the ladle and examined it.

"Were there words on it before?" he asked the three kids.

They crowded around the robot. Junior turned the ladle so they could read the curling words that went down the handle and wrapped around the bowl:

Mission Directions:
Three Earth Children must find
three Fire Children.
Six will go.
Five will return.

"That's creepy," said Polly.

Joe looked over at Junior. "I think this means you have to come with us," he said reluctantly. He'd been looking forward to leaving the pompous robot.

"Oh, no," said Junior. "I've done my part. I helped you come here, risking my life and—"

He broke off as the fire rose up in another shower of sparks, which rained down on him.

"I want to go home," he said miserably.

Sam reached out and touched the robot's arm, which was surprisingly warm. "We need your help," he said. "Don't you see?"

"Junior come, too!" said Dimitri. "Yes?" His eye blinked hopefully under the shaggy brow. "We will have fun."

"Very well," said Junior grumpily. "But don't expect me to be taking care of you."

"We have never asked you to take care of anything," replied Joe. He gritted his teeth.

"I will carry," said Dimitri. He stood up and scooped them all up in his arms like a bundle of dolls. Then he dipped his toe in the fire.

The sea and the volcano shivered and disappeared.

CHAPTER NINE

Olympus

The night sky was much closer. The deep blue was studded with sparkling constellations of people and creatures. The moon was a slice on the horizon carried by a pale girl on a white horse. The air was cool.

The mismatched group was looking over a wall of roses onto velvety grass stretched out in all directions. Deep green bushes were trimmed in the forms of dancing fauns. The tree trunks were shaped like long, lithe ladies. The tree ladies were all asleep, holding their branches over their heads like living lacy umbrellas.

"Home!" cried Junior.

"Not my home," said the Cyclops. He looked around, then crouched down behind the rose wall. Carefully, he lowered them all to the ground. His big toe had nearly put out a small fire contained by a circle of white stones. Polly noticed the stones had little suns carved into them. The Cyclops hurriedly moved his toe.

The three kids looked around. The fire was in the center of an enclosed garden. The garden walls were shaped from rosebushes and the ground was spongy, rich moss. In the calm beauty, Sam, Polly, and Joe suddenly felt exhausted.

"Where are we?" asked Joe.

"Olympus," said Junior. "The home of the gods."

"But *where* in Olympus?" asked Polly.

"I'm not sure," said the robot. "I don't leave the forge here very often," he added defensively.

Sam sat down by the fire, his eyes drooping. Joe knew just how he felt.

"Do you think it is safe to sleep here?" asked Joe.

The robot nodded. "All of Olympus is safe."

"Yeah," said Joe, "if you're a god or immortal or something. But is it safe for *us*?"

Junior shifted uncomfortably. "I should think so," he said.

"I think not so safe for Sam, Polly, Joe, and Dimitri," the Cyclops said. "I will guard." He sat cross-legged on the grass and leaned against one of the high rosebushes. It bent quite a bit.

"Don't knock the wall over," said Polly.

The Cyclops blinked and turned around. "Oh dear," he said, moving away.

"I don't need to sleep," said Junior. "I'm going to go back to the forge."

"But you need to come with us on the mission," protested Sam.

"I will return by dawn," said the robot.

"Promise?" asked Polly.

The robot nodded. He handed Joe the

ladle, then went through the arched entrance to the garden and disappeared into the night.

Polly opened the backpack. "I'm glad we brought food," she said.

"I'm starved," said Joe.

They ate the peanut butter and jelly sandwiches and drank the water they had. Dimitri turned down their offers of food.

"Not hungry," he said.

"Do you think Smith will be worried about you?" asked Joe.

"Smith will know I am with you," said Dimitri. "He will be happy."

"I hope so," said Polly.

Sam fell asleep before he finished his sandwich, curled up on the soft moss beside the warm fire. Polly and Joe weren't far behind him.

The Cyclops watched the stars travel through the quiet night and smiled happily to himself.

Joe woke to a gentle touch on the forehead. He slowly opened his eyes. It was still dark.

A girl with golden skin and curling red hair stood over him. Her mouth was wide and her chin was pointed. Her eyes looked right into Joe's. They were a twinkling light purple that shone even in the flickering firelight.

Joe blinked.

"What a wonderful dream," he said, his voice croaking.

The girl smiled so that her eyes crinkled up. Joe blushed. It wasn't a dream, after all. The memory of the last day came back to him and he slowly sat up. He noticed that he felt refreshed and rested, not as if he'd been sleeping outside on the ground all night.

The girl had moved on and was gently waking Sam. Joe couldn't take his eyes off her. She had on a pink dress that floated around her. He tried to guess how old she was: maybe eighteen or nineteen. Too old to pay attention to him. Joe sighed.

The sky was growing lighter. Sam and Polly both yawned and stretched. The girl stood in front of Dimitri's huge sleeping figure. She had a friendly grin on her face, which made Joe like her even more. She pushed against the Cyclops' leg with both hands. He wouldn't wake up or budge an inch.

The girl pushed again.

"Do you want some help?" Joe asked.

The girl turned and looked at him. "No, thank you. I want to wake him up quietly."

At the sound of voices, the Cyclops' eye opened. "I awake!" he announced guiltily. "I only close eye for small time. But should not have closed eye at all."

"It's okay, Dimitri," said Joe.

Polly and Sam came up and patted the worried-looking giant.

"You kept us safe all night long," said Polly.

"Yeah," said Sam.

Dimitri nodded. His eye shifted to the girl. "Who are you, pretty lady?"

The girl laughed and gave a small bow. "I am Eos," she said. "Also known as Dawn."

"You mean *the* dawn?" asked Polly. "As in when the sun rises?"

"Yes," said Eos. "And who are you?"

The three kids introduced themselves and then Dimitri.

"And why are you here?" Eos asked. "Humans are not meant to come to Olympus. You'll have to leave, and pretty quickly. If someone finds you, I hate to think what would happen. Zeus tosses people down to Earth, Hera turns people into animals, Artemis . . ."

"I get the picture," said Joe. "But I think we need some help, or something, before we go." He proceeded to tell her their story, finishing with the last message on the ladle, which Sam held out.

Eos was looking at the words in the light of the fire when Junior came through the archway. He was carrying a plate piled high with fruit and a glowing pitcher.

"Hello, Junior," said Eos.

"Good morning, Lady Eos," Junior said stiffly. "Have these children told you about this silly adventure?"

Eos nodded. "It's not silly," she said sternly.

"And *I* plan on coming with you. We should leave soon, though."

Junior sighed. Joe found a grin spreading uncontrollably on his face.

"You're really going to come with us?" Polly asked. "Are you one of the Fire Children, too?"

Eos nodded. "Of course. I am the first light of the earth and older sister to Helios, the sun."

"Cool!" said Sam. "What do you think we should do next?"

"I think you should all eat and gather your strength while I ask my brother to take my morning shift in the sky. It will make him grumpy, but he owes me a favor." Eos looked thoughtful for a second. "We will leave as soon as I return. Be as quiet as you can."

"Great!" whispered Joe. "Really great." Then he shrugged his shoulders and tried to be less eager. "I mean, that should work out. I mean, you're a Child of Fire, we need three of them—I mean, you . . ." His voice trailed off.

Polly grinned and nudged Sam. "Joe has a crush on someone," she whispered loudly.

"Do not!" said Joe.

"Shh!" said Eos with a smile.

Joe blushed again. "You shut up!" he whispered fiercely to Polly, who smirked at him.

The three kids and the Cyclops ate the fruit and drank juice from the glowing pitcher as quickly as they could. Everything had an amazing flavor, stronger and longer-lasting than that of regular fruit. And no matter how much they ate, there was more.

Eos returned through the rose arch.

"Ready?" she asked.

"Um, do you think we could, um, visit a bathroom?" asked Polly.

"Oh!" said Eos. "Of course. Let me show you."

She led them to a small marble bathroom outside the garden. Feeling much better, they returned to the garden one by one.

Joe was the last to come back. He had tried to comb his hair back and it hadn't been easy. Even now he could feel it flopping back on his forehead.

The sky was turning pink. They gathered around the fire, the Cyclops crouching by the rose wall to stay hidden.

"Should we use the copper?" asked Joe. "Since it's dawn?"

"Save it," said Eos. "I bet I can make this work." She stepped delicately into the fire and held out her hand.

Joe took it and squeezed it gently.

Just then they heard a voice call out, "Eos, what's going on? Who do you have in there with you?"

Eos gave a hearty tug and Joe walked into the fire. "Take someone's hand, quickly!" Eos said.

Polly took Joe's hand. Then Sam took Polly's and Junior reluctantly took Sam's.

Dimitri came last, holding onto Junior's arm with one finger.

"Eos! I asked you a question!" came the voice faintly through the fire. Then the garden shimmered and was gone.

CHAPTER TEN

Titan

They were at the foot of a high, stony mountain. A cold wind whipped sharply around them. The sky was a uniform gray, which made it impossible to tell what time of day it was. Large rock formations loomed on one side of them. There was no fire.

"Where are we?" asked Sam.

"And why isn't there a fire?" asked Joe, glancing around.

Eos pointed up and opened her mouth to speak.

Then the rocks beside them shifted. A grating sound filled the air as they moved, and rocks began falling alongside the little group. These rocks were clear and strangely shaped in linked loops. They all had to run to get out of the way, even Dimitri.

"Bad mountain!" Dimitri shouted.

The rocks stopped falling.

They slowly came to a halt and looked back. The strange clear pile of rocks had fallen in a heap beside the big rocks that had moved.

"What is that?" asked Sam.

"I believe it is a diamond chain," said Eos.

"A *what*?" asked Joe. He could see the clear rocks made a chain, but surely they were way too big to be made of diamond.

"A diamond chain," Eos repeated. She looked up and took a deep breath. "That's Prometheus. It was his foot that just moved. The diamond chain binds him."

They all looked at the rocks. Slowly, they

could make out the shape of toes and a heel. From there they could see the ankle, with chains wrapped around it.

They all looked higher up the mountain and, now that they knew what they were looking at, they could see a man leaning against the mountain. His hair was steel gray and went past his shoulders. He was dressed in brown-gray clothing the color of dirt-covered stones. His skin was a light, sickly gray.

"Prometheus!" said Polly.

"He's a *giant*," said Sam.

"Bigger than me," said Dimitri in wonder.

"Actually, he's a Titan," said Eos. "They were giants who ruled the earth before the gods and goddesses."

"Kind of like dinosaurs," said Sam.

"Yes," said Eos. "Prometheus gave people fire, and Zeus is punishing him for it. Every day an eagle comes and eats Prometheus' liver."

"Ow!" said Sam.

"Gross!" said Polly.

Eos nodded. "Because Prometheus is immortal, his liver grows back each night. That way the eagle may feed again the following day."

The three kids looked back up at the Titan. His arms were wrapped around the back of the mountain and his face was turned away from them, resting on the mountain peak. They could barely see his chest rising and falling with his breathing.

"This must be why we are here," said Sam.

"Yes," said Eos. "We are Children of Earth and Fire—bound together by Prometheus' actions. Now, together, we can free him."

"I will do it!" said Dimitri. He strode over to the diamond links. Even in *his* hands, they looked big. He tried to pull the links apart. They made a grating sound. Dimitri let out a growl and pulled again. Nothing happened. He gave it one more try, then dropped the chain and hung his head.

"There isn't anything we can do," said Junior fatalistically.

"That's not true," said Polly. "We can't just give up!"

"Let's light a fire," said Joe.

"Let's use the fish!" said Sam.

"The fish?" asked Eos.

Joe pulled off the backpack and dug around in it. He pulled out the fish.

Eos laughed. "Oh, *that* fish! You mean use copper!"

"Yes," said Sam.

"It's not dawn, though," said Junior.

"Eos is dawn lady," said Dimitri, his face brightening.

"Yes!" said Polly. "The message said 'with first light' and we're with her!"

Polly and Sam started hunting for anything that would burn. There wasn't a lot. By the time Joe had found the matchbox, at the very bottom of the backpack, they had a meager pile of dried grass and scrawny twigs.

Joe knelt down and lit one of the matches. Just then there came a loud screech. They looked up to see an eagle the size of a small airplane flapping toward them, a hungry gleam in its eyes.

The grinding sound of the giant shifting filled the air. Then a groan like thunder.

"Duck!" shouted Eos as the eagle swooped down at them, its talons spread wide.

They scattered, running for cover. The matches went flying, the fire forgotten.

Polly felt the wings beating right behind her as she dove behind a thorny bush. Dimitri swatted at the eagle, but it was too fast for his slow swings.

The eagle climbed into the sky and circled back around.

"Why is it bothering with us?" Polly cried. "Isn't it supposed to be torturing Prometheus?"

Joe peered up at the circling bird. "After an eternity of eating liver every day, we must look pretty good."

Suddenly, they all heard a shout.

A streak of gold ran from behind some rocks. It was Junior.

"I'll distract it!" he yelled. "Light the fire! Dimitri, shield the fire from the wind!"

No one moved for a moment; then, as the eagle swooped toward Junior, Eos called out, "Quick! He's giving us a chance."

Dimitri knelt on the rocky ground, holding his arms around the pile of twigs. Eos ran to the shelter he made.

Oh, no, thought Joe as he ran as fast as he could after her. *Junior is sacrificing himself.*

Sam and Polly reached Dimitri's arms a moment later.

The three kids and the youthful goddess gathered around the pitiful pile of twigs. Dimitri sat down and curled over them like a frozen tidal wave.

Frantically, Joe gathered up the fallen matches and matchbox. He tried to get the fire lit, his hands shaking. They could hear Junior shouting and the eagle screeching. Sam and Polly looked out over one of Dimitri's feet.

The gold robot was dashing back and forth,

waving his arms and calling the eagle names. "You can't get me, you old parrot! Parakeet brains! Son of a mangy turkey!"

They watched the eagle dive, and miss. Junior moved very quickly. He ran and dove behind rocks. His shiny body was more dented every time he rose. He was weaving his way up the mountain.

"Let me try," they heard Eos say to Joe.

"Popinjay!" yelled Junior to the eagle. "Half-plucked chicken! Pigeon poop!"

"I want to go help," said Sam, watching the robot's erratic climb.

Polly shook her head. "Junior's a robot; Hephaestus can fix him if the eagle gets him." She fell silent. "At least, I hope he can," she added quietly.

"I got it!" Eos shouted.

When Sam and Polly turned, a little fire crackled in the shelter of Dimitri's body.

"Where's the fish?" shouted Joe as Eos blew on the fire.

They all looked around frantically.

The eagle let out its loudest shriek yet.

A giant yell followed it, a yell that could only have belonged to the Titan.

They turned their gazes to the mountain. The giant's head was raised.

The eagle was flying over them, a golden shape caught in its talons. Even caught, Junior still shouted furiously at it.

As they watched, the eagle deliberately opened its talons. Then Junior was falling through the sky, shouting all the way.

There was a soft thud and then silence.

CHAPTER ELEVEN

Nightmare

The eagle landed beyond them, and they could see bits of gold flying as it tore into the metal.

"I hope it gets sick," said Polly. Her eyes filled with tears. She dashed them away. "It's horrible."

Joe just shook his head. All sorts of emotions welled up, guilt being the biggest one. Guilt for not liking the robot, guilt for not distracting the eagle himself.

Sam just stood with an open mouth.

Dimitri tried to get up. They could hear him gulping back tears. "My brother," he cried. "He was my brother."

Eos shouted, "Find that fish! Don't let Junior's sacrifice be in vain!"

They all hunted through the scattered contents of the backpack to the sound of Dimitri's heavy sobs. Sam found it behind a small rock.

"Hurry!" yelled Eos, who ran to the fire. "The eagle!"

The huge bird had risen again and was winging its way toward them.

Sam felt the beating of the bird's wings as he threw the fish to Eos. Suddenly, Dimitri surged up, his fist knocking the eagle to one side.

The fire danced and grew. Eos caught the copper fish and dropped it right into the leaping flames.

They all froze and stared at the fire, except for Dimitri, who was holding the eagle.

There was a cracking sound. The fire split

in half and a little flame the size of a hummingbird flew up, straight into the air. It rose higher and higher, a bright spot against the gray sky. When it had almost disappeared, it started to fall back to earth, like a small meteor. The flame was heading right for the chained Titan on the mountain.

"*No!*" shouted Joe.

The flame hit the giant man. There was a sound like an explosion; then the mountain gave a lurch and a rain of stones tumbled down from the top.

Dimitri scooped them all up in his arms and ran as the rocks hurtled in their direction.

A screech filled the air. Then the sound of falling stones was replaced with a crackling. Dimitri stopped and turned. A fire was burning on the Titan's chest. The rocks that had fallen had made a giant ring around the mountain.

The eagle circled overhead. It gave one more screech. Then it tipped its wings and flapped away.

Dimitri sank to the ground and lowered Joe, Sam, Polly, and Eos. He had stopped beside what was left of the gold robot.

They sat, huddled together, as the fire grew until it consumed the man on the mountain and the mountain itself. Both flames and smoke stayed within the circle of stones. After a while they gathered the golden shards of metal that had once been Junior. They put them in a pile beside Dimitri, who wouldn't move or speak.

Eos leaned against the Cyclops and put her arms around Joe. Polly leaned against Joe. Sam leaned against Polly, holding her hand, his other hand resting on a piece of gold.

They stayed that way as the sky grew dark and the mountain burned.

Six will go, and five will return, thought Joe as he shut his eyes in exhaustion. *I hope we did what we were supposed to do.*

By the time the clouds cleared, they were all in an uncomfortable sleep. But when the bright stars and the crescent of moon shone down on them, they relaxed, and their night-mares became simple dreams of home and comfort.

Dimitri and Eos woke Sam, Polly, and Joe with shouts. Eos was standing with her arms raised over her head, waving. Dimitri was waving and calling, "Here we be! Here we be!"

A bright young man was coming out of the night sky in a silver chariot drawn by pastel-colored horses. He looked very annoyed. Smith sat beside him, grinning and waving.

"Who's that with Smith?" Sam asked sleepily.

"My brother, Helios," said Eos. "He has brought me my chariot."

The chariot alighted, and the man jumped out. Behind it another set of horses, these deep gold, landed with a chariot of the same color. They lit the air with bright light.

"It took us practically all night to find you," Helios said. "And we only did because the moon saw you." Eos hugged him. He went on, but in a lighter tone, "You owe *me* now."

Eos smiled. "We'll see how long that lasts! I bail you out all the time."

Dimitri had gathered Junior's broken parts in one hand and run over to the chariot where Smith sat. He knelt beside the chariot and began telling Smith everything that had happened. Huge tears rolled out of his one eye, making salty puddles on the ground.

Smith nodded and listened to every word. His face was sad and tired. When Dimitri finished talking, Smith put his hands on the Cyclops' arm. He said something too softly for anyone but Dimitri to hear.

Eos brought Sam, Polly, and Joe forward. "These are my friends," she said to Helios.

Helios glared at them. "They're the ones who got you into trouble, huh?"

Eos just laughed again. "I'm afraid it might be the other way around," she said.

Smith then called them over. He gave them all hugs. Then, smiling mysteriously, he brought out a small bag. He handed it to Joe. "I think you will be needing these."

"What about Junior?" asked Polly.

"Will he be okay?" asked Sam.

Smith nodded. "I think that Dimitri and I can rebuild him together. I have a feeling that this whole experience will have changed him quite a bit."

"You should be proud of him," said Joe.

"I am," said Smith. "Without him Prometheus would not be free. And the fire would not be happy."

"Is Prometheus really free, then?" asked Joe.

"From what I understand, you hatched a phoenix in the fire," explained Smith. "When it dove into Prometheus' heart, it gave him the power to be born again in the fire. Fire has the power to destroy and to create."

Smith smiled gently at their still concerned faces. "You'll see," he said. "I promise." He nodded to Helios.

The bright god grinned. "Yeah, you guys get to come with me. My sis will take Smith home ahead of us."

"What about Dimitri?" asked Sam.

"He's going to walk home," said Smith.

Dimitri nodded. "I like to walk."

The mountain was a black shadow against the purpling sky. All the fires were out.

"We'd better go," said Eos. "It's time to rise and shine!"

Sam, Polly, and Joe hugged Eos, Smith, and Dimitri good-bye.

Eos climbed into the silver chariot with Smith. Helios got into the golden chariot. Sam, Polly, and Joe climbed in beside him. He made them all feel a little shy. Dimitri was waiting for everyone to take off safely before beginning his underground journey.

Eos' pastel horses swooped off the ground. As they rose they began to glow. Dawn light filled the sky.

Joe sighed. Maybe he'd meet another girl like her one day.

"Hang on!" said Helios.

The golden horses ran forward, skimming the dark ground, pulling the chariot behind them. Faster and faster they went toward the horizon. Then the horses leaped and rose into the sky. They banked around to follow the dawn with daylight. All the way across the sky, they could see the moon.

"Look down," said Helios.

The three kids looked down. The earth was far below.

Helios pulled the reins and the horses dove. In the daylight, they could see a tiny Dimitri waving frantically at them beside a green mountain. It was covered with trees. The green mountain glittered as if it had been sprinkled with diamond dust. Tiny rainbows were reflected everywhere. Around the mountain grew a ring of sunflowers, so big the kids could make them out from the air.

"Look closely," said Helios.

In the orangey pink glow of dawn, they could see the shape of a giant man beneath the blanket of green, his chest rising and falling.

"Is it Prometheus?" asked Sam.

Helios nodded. "Yes. Thanks to you, he is

at last allowed to sleep until his children are in desperate need once again."

"Wow," said Polly.

Joe felt the same but didn't say it.

Helios smiled at them. "The gods owe you, more than once by my understanding. Don't forget that. And now I think it's time to take you back to where you belong."

"I forgot my backpack," said Joe.

"Too late," said Helios as the horses streaked across the sky.

Epilogue

*T*hree young people walk out of the sun onto a green meadow. It is noon. They are greeted by laughing parents and smiling relatives.

Later, the youngest one opens a black bag. He hands his brother the items inside: a silver ladle, a golden earring, and a copper fish.

There is one more thing inside the bag. It is a small iron box. On its lid shine four designs made of sparkling jewels: an emerald leaf, a turquoise dolphin, a ruby sun, and a diamond feather.

The sister gently lifts the box's lid. Inside is a miniature scroll tied with a gold ribbon. The oldest brother carefully unties the ribbon and unrolls the parchment. It flutters in the wind, tiny words dancing across its surface:

You never know . . .

Read all four books in

The Magic Elements Quartet

MALLORY LOEHR lives in Brooklyn, New York, but grew up all over the world. The one constant place in her life has been her grandparents' farm in Virginia, where campfires are commonplace on cool summer nights. Some of her favorite authors growing up were (and still are!) Diana Wynne Jones, Lloyd Alexander, and Edward Eager. Ms. Loehr loves to read, write, play the piano, and dance the tango. She is also the lucky person who gets to edit such fabulous writers as Mary Pope Osborne and Tamora Pierce. And she has a fireplace in her apartment.

A STEPPING STONE BOOK™

Great authors write great books...
for fantastic first reading experiences!

Grades 1–3

Duz Shedd series
   by Marjorie Weinman Sharmat
Junie B. Jones series by Barbara Park
Magic Tree House® series
   by Mary Pope Osborne
Marvin Redpost series by Louis Sachar

Clyde Robert Bulla
The Chalk Box Kid
The Paint Brush Kid
White Bird

Jackie French Koller
Mole and Shrew Are Two
Mole and Shrew All Year Through
Mole and Shrew Have Jobs to Do

Jerry Spinelli
Tooter Pepperday
Blue Ribbon Blues: A Tooter Tale

Grades 2–4

A to Z Mysteries® series by Ron Roy
The Katie Lynn Cookie Company series
   by G. E. Stanley

Polly Berrien Berends
The Case of the Elevator Duck

Ann Cameron
Julian, Dream Doctor
Julian, Secret Agent
Julian's Glorious Summer

Adèle Geras
Little Swan

**Stephanie Spinner &
Jonathan Etra**
Aliens for Breakfast
Aliens for Lunch
Aliens for Dinner

Gloria Whelan
Next Spring an Oriole
Silver
Hannah
Night of the Full Moon
Shadow of the Wolf

Grades 3–5

FICTION
The Magic Elements Quartet
   by Mallory Loehr
#1: Water Wishes
#2: Earth Magic
#3: Wind Spell
#4: Fire Dreams

Spider Kane Mysteries
   by Mary Pope Osborne
#1: Spider Kane and the Mystery Under the
   May-Apple
#2: Spider Kane and the Mystery at Jumbo
   Nightcrawler's

NONFICTION
Thomas Conklin
The *Titanic* Sinks!

Elizabeth Cody Kimmel
Balto and the Great Race

Want to know more about Greek myths?
Read
D'Aulaires' Book of Greek Myths
and
The Random House Book of Greek Myths

At first Toots thought it was
a trick of the light.

She screwed up her eyes, then opened them wide, but it was still there. High in the corner of the ceiling a tiny door had opened, and a creature, no more than half an inch high, had climbed through. Toots could see it as clearly as she could see the books on the bookshelves. The creature was crossing the ceiling and making its way toward the brass lamp in the center, leaving a trail of dark, smudgy footprints on the clean white paint as it did so.

Discover a hidden world above and beyond the ceiling of your living room in *Toots and the Upside-Down House* **by Carol Hughes.**